To my family, for all your support

&

Deana Bojkovski, My Editor

O: Finn

Thanks for READING ME!

Pork Chop!

Princess Panda
and the
Loyal Order of the Boomerdogs

Volume 1

On a warm and sunny, spring day, Mr. Bear's daughter, Amanda, brought home a beautiful, little puppy, a black and white "teacup" Pomeranian female. She had soft black and white hair with some red fur around her nose; she was barely five pounds, and she could fit right into Mr. Bear's big hand.

"What's her name?" questioned Mr. Bear. "We haven't given her a name yet" said Amanda. "She is so soft and furry, like a little puff-ball, maybe, we should name her Puff-Ball." Amanda said.

"Well, we have plenty of time to name her, right now I am hoping she will not be afraid of Big Boomer." the big, yellow, lab that lived with Mr. Bears family on Grosse Ile (the "Big Island" in French).

Big Boomer was the family dog and had been for the last 12 years. He wasn't called a Labrador Retriever, but he was a "Boomerdog," the name Mr. Bear liked to use instead of "Labrador Retriever" to Mr. Bear, all yellow labs were "Boomerdogs."

Just then, a big, yellow snout with a pink nose at the very end came sniffing into the room, it was Big Boomer.

He kept his nose low and sniffed as he came into any room, which he did to find any hidden treats that may have fallen off of someones plate the night before.

Suddenly, Boomers head went straight up as he smelled a smell that he hadn't before. He picked up the scent of the puppy even before he saw her.

"What's this," laughed Boomer as he gazed down on the tiny puppy. "I've never seen a puppy so small" said Big Boomer. He bent way over and lowered his nose to the baby Pomeranian. "Hello, little dog; don't be afraid, no one will hurt you, my name is Boomer and you can call me Big Boomer, like everyone else."

"Alright, thank you," said the little pup in a low, soft voice. She was trembling a little "you are all very nice, but I miss my mama and my brothers and sisters. Can I go home now? I miss my family..."

"You are home little pup," exclaimed Big Boomer. "You're in our family; Mr. Bear's family I mean. You're gonna live here with me and Mr. Bear and Amanda and Mrs. Rabbit. We are your family now little pup."

With that, the tiny Pomeranian puppy laid down into a tiny ball of fur and cried, and she cried some more until she fell asleep; she was exhausted.

"Let her sleep awhile Boomer," said Mr. Bear. Then he picked up his keys and went out the door. "We'll see you later after the show Boomer, you look after the new dog ok, boy?"

Boomer barked back, "ok, Mr. Bear."

Boomer walked back to the sleeping ball of fur. "Really cute little dog," he thought. Boomer circled around two times before he laid down, putting the pup near his belly, and surrounding her with his massive body.

Several hours later, a storm came raging into Grosse Ile from out of Lake Erie, the lightning flashed and the thunder boomed. Many adult dogs are afraid of storms, but to a six week old puppy in a strange house on the first night, it was terribly frightening.

Boomer wasn't afraid of thunder and lightning, Boomer wasn't afraid of much anything except missing a meal or worse, a treat. He walked over to the little dog and looked into her dark, tiny eyes, "don't be afraid little pup, it's only a storm, it'll stop in a couple of minutes." But the thunder grew even louder and the lightning closer together, the storm was raging.

Boomer had an idea, he always loved it when Mr. Bear would tell him a story; maybe he could tell a story to the pup.

"Little pup, listen up. If you quit crying and settle down, I'll tell you a story my mom used to tell me when I was a little pup." Boomer whispered softly.

"You were little too!" said the pup, almost in disbelief. She couldn't even imagine such a big dog as Big Boomer could have ever been little like her.

"Now get your little self-comfortable and cozy, and I'll begin the story," Boomer said, as he curled up even tighter around the small dog.

"Once upon a time a..." The puppy was pulling on

Big Boomers tail, interrupting him.

"What's the name of the story Big Boomer? What's the name, so I can remember to ask for it again?"

"The name of the story is "Princess Panda and the Loyal Order of the Boomerdogs." Now, no more questions until after I tell the story."

"Once upon a time there was a kingdom that was ruled by King Bear. King Bear was a kindly king who made sure that all of the children of the kingdom were well fed and taken care of. The people all loved King Bear and his queen, Queen Rabbit. The king and the queen had one child, the precious Princess Panda.

Princess Panda was seven years old and the pride and joy of her parents, and she, of course; loved them back just as much.

The king and his royal family were guarded not by soldiers who could fall asleep on duty, or worse; run away when you needed them. No, the royal family was guarded by a platoon of guard dogs. All of the guard dogs were Boomerdogs (yellow Labrador Retrievers). The Boomerdogs were led by the biggest and most reliable of all the Boomerdogs. The captain of the Boomerdogs was the lead dog.

All of the Boomerdogs had the same heavy-duty collars of leather and silver. They wore helmets of polished steel and they all had long, flowing capes that stuck out to their tails. The capes were yellow and purple, the royal colors, and the royal seal of two great bears holding the globe was embroidered into the center of the cape.

All of the collars had a silver star impressed into it, all that is except one; the captains seal. The captain's seal was solid gold and was only for the captain of the guard dogs.

The king and queen were attending to a state dinner and had to go into town, they told Princess Panda to stay on the castle grounds and not to wander into the woods. There was a tale of a large wolf pack, led by a huge, silver backed wolf.

Princess Panda longed to get out of the courtyard and explore the world outside, it wouldn't be that bad, she thought. She knew she wouldn't be able to climb over it, and she couldn't dig under it. She walked along the edges of the courtyard until she spied a gate in the fence on the back of the property. The gate had a lock but Princess Panda knew there was a key ring in the tool shed. She stealthily snuck into the shed, stole the keys, and opened the locked gate. She ran out to the path with the gate swinging behind her.

Back in the palace, the dog guards didn't notice anything amiss, since Princess Panda always spent most of the day in the garden in the courtyard, surrounded by all her favorite flowers.

Princess Panda was running down the path into the woods with great expectations to see new and wondrous things, but all she saw was the same old woods that all looked alike to her, and what's worse she was lost, she took the right fork in the path or was it the left. And it was getting dark soon.

The pack was headed up the mountains for prey, they were looking for deer or stray livestock to feed upon, it had been several days since they've eaten anything, and they were getting dangerously close to the castle grounds.

Heading up the pack was a huge, silver gray wolf, the alpha male of the pack. Being the alpha male meant that the silver wolf was the leader of the pack, and to disobey him meant a good bite in the rump or worse. The silver wolf scanned the air for the scent of prey; deer, or a warren of rabbits could be on the menu. Suddenly, the silver-backed wolf turned north towards the castle and its garden.

Princess Panda meanwhile was hopelessly lost. When she thought she was headed back to the castle, she was actually going away from it; towards the wolves who had already smelled the Princess and were closing in on her.

The Princess was actually going around the edge of the castle grounds, wandering in circles until she looked through the leaves and saw the castle on the other side of the glade; she cried out with joy as she ran into the field of grass and ran straight to the garden of the castle; she could see the back gate she foolishly opened when she sneaked out.

The pack had circled around and anticipated the child would run across the glade at the spot she did; the lead wolf, the silver one, was staying back and letting the other dogs in the pack make the kill; he will, of course, eat his full before any of them will so much as take a bite.

Princess Panda suddenly looked up and saw the wolf pack. She turned and screamed, running back the other way, away from the pack. She ran with all of her might, but the pack was easily catching up to her, they would have her in seconds.

Then, just as Princess Panda thought the wolves would be upon her, she saw a flash of purple and yellow, the royal colors, and she saw the outline of the two great bears holding the globe, the Loyal Order of Boomerdogs. The guard dogs had come to save her.

"Circle the princess," barked out the leader of the Boomerdogs to the others, "Attack the wolves in pairs like you have trained." commanded the lead dog, the lead dog with the golden buckle.

At his command a handful of the biggest Boomerdogs circled around Princess Panda, protecting her with their huge bodies while snarling at the wolf pack with snapping jaws and sharp teeth.

The other Boomerdogs attacked the wolves in pairs, two against one, the other wolves ran and were confused by the tactic. The pack was running away when suddenly; the silver wolf growled at the rest of the pack, "Come back you cowards, come back," but the pack still ran leaving the silver wolf to snatch the child and run.

The alpha wolf turned toward the child. He saw the guard dogs surrounding her, but what made up his mind was the lead Boomerdog with the gold buckle on his collar. The captain of the Boomerdogs came from behind the other dogs, fearlessly charging at the now lone, silver wolf.

In a flash as quick as he came, the alpha wolf was gone and the princess was saved. They went back to the castle where a grateful King Bear and Queen Rabbit embraced their little girl. "And they all lived happily ever after," said Big Boomer to the small puppy as she stretched about the floor.

Big Boomer looked at the puppy as she stretched, with her small nose on one end, and her fluffy, Pomeranian tail on the other, he knew that the outline of the little dog reminded him of something. "That's it," he exclaimed. Boomer couldn't help to think she looked like an outline of a pork chop walking across the floor, "That's it, we will call you Pork Chop. Pup, that is your new name." "Pork Chop it is," laughed Big Boomer.

The storm had passed during the telling of the story and the two dogs, now good friends, lay down for the night. Big Boomer curled up like a ball and Pork Chop, the newly named Pomeranian puppy, snuggled up to Boomers belly and laid her little head upon his huge paws and both went to sleep.

TWO YEARS LATER...

Pork Chop was now the big dog of the house. Boomer had gotten sick a couple months ago and was gone; Pork Chop missed him so much and thought about him every day. She would want him to be proud of her as she tried to take his place as guardian of Mr. Bear's house.

Dogs grow up much quicker than children. It is because of this, that at two years old, Pork Chop was almost an adult, even if she weighed a feather over six pounds. She patrolled the house at night like she had seen Big Boomer do countless times before, sniffing around every door and window, and as everyone knows, dogs are naturally very nosey creatures. It's in their blood.

Pork Chop made her rounds around the dimly lit house and spied a box in the corner of the pantry by the closet. The box was polished wood with the outline of two large bears on their hind legs holding a globe of the Earth between them overhead. Someone must have just put this box out while cleaning the pantry. She knew she would have noticed it before.

Pork Chop nudged the box open with her nose, springing back the lid; she pulled out a delicate cape, half purple and half gold. Beneath the royal cape was a leather collar with a bright, golden buckle and a gold star set upon it saying, "Big Boomer, Captain of the Boomerdogs."

"Big Boomer, you really were the hero after all," she cried, "you will always be my hero," she said. The tears welled up in her eyes. "Goodbye, my best friend," she sobbed, as she closed her eyes and went to sleep.

The End

You're too little, little, little

Volume 2

Pork Chop was a small teacup Pomeranian. She was called teacup because that is the smallest of the breed. She weighed about six pounds, was black and white, and had reddish fur on her cheeks.

Because she was so small, she was the runt of the litter, which means she was the smallest dog of all her brothers and sisters.

Pork Chop lived in a house on a hill that overlooked the river. She lived there with her master, Mr. Bear, and his wife, Mrs. Rabbit.

The river surrounded the house, because the house was on an island. The island was called 'Grosse Ile,' that's a french word for 'Big Island.'

The woods behind the house were deep and large, full of pines and cedars and oaks and many other trees that she didn't know, but what Pork Chop did know was that the woods were dark even during the day, and besides, she wasn't allowed to go into the woods.

Mr. Bear said that there were too many critters in the woods that could hurt or even eat a small dog. Things like coyotes and raccoons or even hawks and eagles lived on the island.

Pork Chop had friends that lived next door, there

was Riff, the one hundred pound German police dog. Riff and Pork Chop were good buddies, Riff was always looking out for Pork Chop like a big friend.

There was also old Barney and mean Cindy. Old Barney was a very old black and white Cocker Spaniel. He moved very slow and mostly just laid in the shade all day.

Mean Cindy was a coal black Scottie dog with a mean streak, especially to Pork Chop. She was much bigger than Pork Chop weighing maybe twenty pounds.

Mean Cindy liked to bite both people and animals. She would wait until someone turned around and would run up and bite them. Pork Chop was afraid of her. If it wasn't for Riff, the one hundred pound German police dog, Pork Chop was sure that mean Cindy would bite her and beat her up, But Riff would always protect her, he was after all; a police dog and even mean Cindy wouldn't dare bite him.

Next door to Pork Chops house, the neighbor had a baby girl named Gracie. Gracie was a beautiful blond baby girl with bright, pretty blue eyes. She was always watched by her nanny. Nanny Logan was a portly, jolly women with flush pink cheeks and a ready smile as broad as her round face. Nanny Logan loved all the animals, especially dogs, and of course, she loved Pork Chop most of all.

That particular afternoon baby Grace was in the back of the house lying on a big, blue blanket on the grass. Pork Chop ran over to the next yard, as she always did, and she laid down on the blanket next to Grace; Nanny Logan was laying down on the blanket. She wasn't moving, she didn't even get up when Gracie started moving around.

Pork Chop tried to wake up Nanny Logan, "BARK,

BARK, BARK," said Pork Chop, "Wake Up." But Nanny Logan still didn't move, Pork Chop was confused; then baby Gracie started to run.

Grace ran like the 2 year old she was, wobbling side to side, as one foot kept stepping past the other. She laughed as she ran, giggling; she thought they were playing a game.

Pork Chop looked over to Nanny Logan and barked her loudest bark, "BARK, BARK, BARK!" she screamed. Nanny Logan still didn't move.

Pork Chop didn't know what to do. As she turned back to baby Grace, she saw the child running through the yard and towards the woods.

"Not the woods," cried Pork Chop, but Gracie kept laughing and she kept running; running deeper and deeper into the woods.

Pork Chop had to stop Grace from going into the woods, but she wasn't allowed out of the yard, what to do, she thought, she didn't want to disobey, but she had to protect the baby so she ran through the yard chasing Grace, who was now across the yard and well into the woods.

Back in the woods, well ahead of Pork Chop and Grace, deep in the green leaves were three pairs of yellow eyes peering at them, watching them, following them as the pair wandered through the trees.

The three pairs of eyes belonged to three coyotes. There was Rax, the biggest coyote; he was an Apex Predator. An Apex Predator is the biggest, meanest, and most dangerous. He had two followers, one was Rump because he was fat, and the other coyote was Runt because he was the smallest. Rump and Runt did everything Rax told them to do. Rax could be very mean to them if they disobeyed; he would bite them on their backs and butts if he was mad; they were afraid of him.

Now, back at the yard, Riff; the one hundred pound German police dog was playfully snapping at a butterfly that was flying around his head.

Riffs' pen was very large for just one dog, even a large dog like him. There was a large oak tree at one end of the pen that had cool shade for most of the day, and a large washtub full of cool water.

Riffs' pen was surrounded by a six foot fence that was set on metal poles. The fence was more to keep coyotes and raccoons out than keep Riff in. Riff was a trained police dog that obeyed all sorts of commands; he wasn't the type of dog that would jump the fence.

Meanwhile, Baby Grace was getting tired and she started to cry. Pork Chop tried to cuddle with her and to calm her down, she had always liked it when Pork Chop would lick her face. But not today, Gracie cried even louder for her Nanny Logan. Neither Pork Chop or Grace knew that the three coyotes were watching their every move.

Rax, the Apex Predator, sniffed the air around him as he would always do before he stalked his prey. He smelled Pork Chop, he had smelled her before when she walked by the woods edge. But he thought this other smell is different; it is a human, but it smells different.

Rax was curious now about baby Grace, he jumped out of the bushes and walked right up to baby Grace. He lowered his head and sniffed at the baby's diaper, and then her hair. Grace was frightened, she was used to dogs, even big Riff, but the sight of Rax made her cry even louder.

Pork Chop ran up to Rax and barked to him "Leave the baby alone Rax! We are lost and I have to take care of her."

Rax thundered back to Pork Chop. "Who do you think you are little pet dog? Do you think you can stop me? Who's going to take care of you?"

Pork Chop backed away from Rax, he was huge; almost as big as Riff, the one hundred pound German police dog. She was very afraid but she was even more afraid for baby Grace.

"Oh," thought Pork Chop, "What can I do? I'm not big like Riff, I'm just little, little, little." Pork Chop looked about and saw a pile of lumber that was stacked in a messy pile, and then, she had a great idea.

"Hey Rax, I'm not afraid of you and your two stupid friends." cried Pork Chop. "You sure are a fat dog Rump," Pork Chop yelled to Rump.

"And your other friend is the smallest coyote I've ever seen; he looks more like a cat than a coyote," Pork Chop said about Runt.

Rax could hardly believe his ears. He was going to leave the baby alone and teach the little dog a lesson.

"Rump, Runt," Rax called to his pack. "Get that little pet dog. Get that little pet dog, and tear her to pieces."

Pork Chop ran to the pile of lumber with the

coyote's right on her tail. She jumped in between the logs just as the snapping jaws clicked behind her.

Pork Chop backed up in the pile of logs, she just fit in between them; the other dogs were too large to reach in to get her. Pork Chops plan had worked! She was always too little and now being too little is a good thing.

The dogs barked and howled. Rax was furious and he pushed the other dogs out of the way and snarled at Pork Chop. "I'm still going to get you, little pet dog." he said. And with that he began to dig under the wood pile just as fast as he could; the other dogs joined in too. It wouldn't be too long before they could dig into Pork Chops hiding spot.

Pork Chop was frightened, more frightened than ever before. The coyotes were almost into the pile of logs; she didn't know what to do. She started crying and then she started screaming...

"HELP, OH! HELP ME SOMEBODY PLEASE, HELP ME!" cried the little dog.

"RIFF, RIFF, PLEASE COME AND HELP ME! PLEASE RIFF, PLEASE" She yelled at the top of her lungs.

Riff, the one hundred pound German police dog had grown tired of the butterflies and was about to lay down in the shade of the tree when suddenly he heard something.

Riffs ears stood straight up and turned toward the sound. Somebody is calling for help, he could hear someone was in trouble because of his police dog training.

He listened as close as he could when suddenly his

eyes grew wide and his heart beat quickly. It was Pork Chops voice he heard. It was Pork Chop who was in trouble!

Now Riff was a good dog, a highly trained police dog, he knew he wasn't supposed to leave his pen, but he had to help Pork Chop, his little friend.

"IM COMING PORK CHOP, IM COMING." barked Riff in his deep, big dog voice. "WOOF, WOOF, WOOF," He commanded. Then in one quick move, he leapt over the fence and ran to baby Gracie's house.

Riff put his head down to pick up the scent as he ran towards Nanny Logan. He licked her face over and over, but she didn't move. Riff knew she needed help. He put his huge head down and picked up Pork Chop and the babies scent. He ran towards the woods and as he rushed he could also smell the scent of the coyotes!

"Rax! That's Rax's smell," Riff said to himself and then he ran even faster.

Runt and Rump had almost gotten into the pile as Pork Chop tried to stay back away from their jaws. She crouched even lower but she knew they were almost upon her.

Riff, the one hundred pound German police dog, bounded up over the ridge towards Rax, who was standing in front of the pile of logs.

Rax bared his considerable teeth, "Go and mind your own business, police dog; this doesn't concern you" he snarled.

But, Big Riff, the one hundred pound German police dog, didn't say anything. He just ran down the hill with his head down and his broad shoulders low. He barreled into Rax and knocked him backwards into the swampy grass.

Rax jumped to his feet in an instant. He was after all, an Apex Predator. He was fully capable of fighting and even killing a big dog like Riff. But today was different. Rax looked into Riffs eyes and saw they were full of fire; Riff was ready for a fight.

Rax hesitated, then he smelled something, something he rarely smelled, something he did not like.

It was fear. Rax could smell his own fear and so could the other dogs. Rax was afraid of Riff.

"Let's get out of here," barked Rax to Rump and Runt. They also could smell the fear in Rax, but they obeyed even as they slyly laughed to each other.

"That little pet dog is not worth our effort," Rax mumbled as the trio slinked away. The coyotes jumped back into the woods just as two policemen came jogging over the hill.

"Did you see that pack of coyotes?" One officer said to the other. "These two dogs must of chased them away just in time," He said gesturing towards Pork Chop and Riff.

The policemen took baby Grace back to the house as the two dogs ran along side. As they got back to the house, they saw the ambulance and the rescue team. The paramedics were loading Nanny Logan onto a stretcher and off to the hospital where she recovered a few days later. Luckily for Nanny, another neighbor saw what she first thought was a pile of clothes laying in the yard. She called 911.

Everybody in the neighborhood knew that Riff and Pork Chop were heroes. They had saved baby Grace from the coyotes, while Nanny Logan had a stroke. Everyone was happy for them; everyone but mean Cindy who was so jealous, she couldn't stand it. He couldn't stand all the attention the little dog was getting.

Pork Chop didn't care what mean Cindy thought, she was just glad that they were all ok and safe. She was also happy that Nanny was ok. But the thing that she was most happy about was that Riff, the one hundred pound German police dog, had come to save her when she really needed him. He was her best friend.

Baby Graces parents came home early and were relieved that no harm had come to Grace. They both took turns hugging her and each other, and they brought a reward for the hero dogs that only hero dogs would get; a huge bowl of beef chunks hand cut by the butcher for Riff, and a medium sized bowl for Pork Chops favorite treat; teddy grams, those little teddy bear cereal cookies that Pork Chop just loved.

And with that the two friends laid next to each other on the cool grass in the big, green yard.

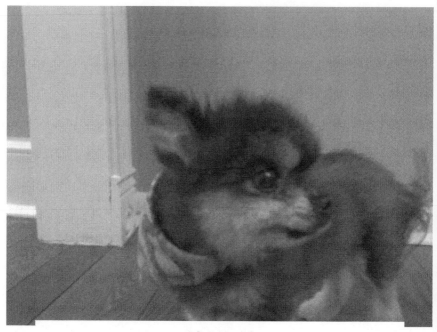

The End

Pork Chop and the Two Tigers

Volume 3

Our story begins just after Christmas on Grosse Ile; "The Big Island." The Christmas tree was still up with all the lights and ornaments. The toys were still under the tree between playtimes, but all of the boxes and wrappers were long gone.

Pork Chop was busy under the tree looking at the mirror on the blue angel ornament. Pork Chop did not know what a mirror was, but she was absolutely fascinated by its reflection. She was standing up on the top of her paws, on her tiptoes, and she was peeking into the almost too high thing of interest. She could see herself in the mirror. "Is that what I look like?" thought the little dog.

Pork Chop was so busy looking at herself she didn't notice that she was sliding into the tree. BANG!! Went the blue angel ornament as it smashed onto the floor. Pork Chop ran under the couch, where she always runs when she is frightened.

Just then at the door, Mr. Bear was bringing in groceries to put on the kitchen table. Mr. Bear looked down at the broken ornament. The blue angel was Mr. Bear's favorite, given to him by Grandma Bear. He looked very sad.

Pork Chop was still under the couch, she was embarrassed and afraid to tell Mr. Bear what happened, she did not move a muscle.

"Hello, Hello is anybody home?"
"Pork Chop, are you in the kitchen?" asked Mr. Bear as he walked around the room to set the groceries down.

"Pork Chop, what happened to the blue angel? Why did it fall down? Where are you, Pork Chop?"

Pork Chop had an idea. She walked slowly out from under the couch, yawning and stretching, just like she had been fast asleep.

"What's all the racket about? I was just taking a nap." Said Pork Chop. "What happened to the blue angel Mr. Bear?" asked Pork Chop with a sheepish look upon her face.

"You mean you don't know who broke it?" asked Mr. Bear to Pork Chop.

Pork Chop hesitated to answer. She already pretended that she didn't see it and now she has to keep lying about it. She thought to herself.

"I was sleeping under the couch when I woke up to a boom and then you walked in the door." Pork Chop said to Mr. Bear, being careful not to look him in the eyes.

"Well perhaps it fell from the rush of air as I opened the door; I was in a hurry to get in, it is freezing outside," exclaimed Mr. Bear.

"Anyway," exclaimed Mr. Bear, "I brought back five cookies from Grandma Bear. I am going to put them on the counter up here," said Mr. Bear. Mr. Bear laid the bag of cookies on the counter, next to the garbage can. He then reached down and handed a whole cookie to Pork Chop. "Here Pork Chop, it's a Pizzelle," laughed Mr. Bear

Pizzelles were one of Pork Chops favorite foods. Grandma Bear made them a couple times a year, but always at Christmas. Pork Chop took the cookie in her mouth, and without savoring it; gobbled it down in a couple of bites like any dog would do a treat.

"Enjoy that cookie," said Mr. Bear. "Remember the ones on the counter are mine, so do not even think about it while I am out on my walk." With that Mr. Bear closed the door behind him, his footfalls distinctly heard all the way down the deck to the road. Pork Chop was alone once again.

"Don't even think about it," said Pork Chop. "How can I think about anything else?" She was actually drooling, she wanted the Pizzelles so much.

Next to the counter was an old box full of junk Mr. Bear was going to throw away. Next to it was the garbage can with the swinging lid, Pork Chop climbed up the top of the upside down box and steadied her paw against the garbage can.

Pork Chop leaned her head towards the bag of Pizzelles and gently pulled at it with her teeth, she was just about to grab them when the top of the box caved in and she caught the lid of the garbage can as she fell.

The Pizzelles, the garbage can, the box, and Pork

Chop came tumbling down with a crash, *BOOM!*

The kitchen was a mess, with most of the garbage laying all about the floor. Pork Chop didn't know where to begin to clean up, and she couldn't reach the counter anyway. The Pizzelles were crushed in the opened bag and the almost empty can of milk leaked into it. They were ruined.

Mr. Bear walked in and saw Pork Chop laying in the middle of the floor amongst the trash.

"Pork Chop, what's is going on? I leave you alone and you tear up the garbage; where's the Pizzelles? *PORK CHOP!*" said Mr. Bear with a shocked look on his face.

Pork Chop was nearly caught red-handed, but she did not want Mr. Bear to know what she did. So she lied once again.

"I was trying to put some garbage away in the can, but I am too small. So, I climbed up on the box." Exclaimed Pork Chop. "I must have grabbed at the Pizzelles when I was falling."

"You must have grabbed them when you were falling?" mumbled Mr. Bear. "Was this before or after you were reaching for them?" He said...." Oh, forget it anyway, I'm much too tired to argue about it." Exclaimed Mr. Bear, and with that, he went off for a nap.

The next day Pork Chop was up early. She was lying on the couch next to where Mr. Bear plays his video games on the Xbox and WII. Pork Chop didn't understand the game or how it was played. She would slap her paw at the controller, if someone left the TV on and it would move the image in the screen.

To Pork Chop this seemed like magic. She was very fascinated by it. She was pawing at the screen. Pork Chop was supposed to clean her toys and her dog bed, as she did every Tuesday. Mr. Bear hadn't come home from work yet and besides, he came home late on Tuesday, so instead of doing her chores like she was supposed to, she batted the game controllers about, going from one to the other; she was lost with time and forgot about Mr. Bear coming home.

Mr. Bear opened the door with a start, as he turned towards the family room, his normally happy face turned ashen and then bright red.

"Pork Chop, you didn't do your chores, did you?" Mr. Bear said in a deep and almost angry voice. As he waited for an answer, Pork Chop stammered and stuttered back and forth, never daring to look into Mr. Bears eyes; brown eyes, that were always round and kind and understanding were now stormy and distant. Pork Chop felt terrible, but she still told another lie.

"Mr. Bear, Mr. Bear you just missed it. There was a big tiger in the back yard just a minute ago and I chased him away." Exclaimed Pork Chop breathlessly as if she was chasing a big tiger.

"A tiger, really...Pork Chop?" said Mr. Bear with a deepening voice.

"Well," said Pork Chop sensing that Mr. Bear didn't believe her. "But...But, there were two big tigers Mr. Bear" Pork Chop said with a braking, high-pitched voice.

"Two tigers?" Mr. Bear started to laugh, but then

his face quickly grew stern. "Two tigers, in my yard, in my neighborhood, surely someone would have seen them or at least their tracks in the fresh snow." Growled Mr. Bear to Pork Chop.

"Maybe, they wrapped their paws with cloth so no one would know they were here." Offered Pork Chop, her face turned in absolute shame, afraid to look at Mr. Bear at all.

"That's it!" yelled Mr. Bear. "That's the last straw. Pork Chop, I am giving you a time out!!"

Pork Chop knew what that meant, 30 minutes in the back yard, rain or shine was bad enough in the summer, but in the cold Michigan winters, it was no fun.

"Out you go, cold air or not," scowled Mr. Bear as he opened the door and pointed outside.

Pork Chop slowly walked out the door into the frozen grass. She hated frozen grass, because it was sharp on her toes as she crunched towards the end of the path and lied down.

In the back of the yard, at the edge of the woods, a pale and mangy coat was lying close to the ground, like a large dog on its belly; but that was no dog, it was Rax the coyote, the Apex Predator, and he was getting closer and closer.

Pork Chop was trying to make the best of her time out as she looked up from the ground and thought she saw something moving in the weeds.

"Hello...hello," said Pork Chop politely. She knew

that someone or something was back there but she couldn't tell who. Whatever it was it had mottled, brown and black coating. Pork Chop could make out a sharp pair of ears covered in fur, kind of like...a coyote!

"It looked like a coyote. It was a coyote!" thought Pork Chop. "It was Rax! The Apex Predator and no friend of hers!!"

A pair of yellow eyes peered through the grass and looked straight at Pork Chop. "Well, what do we have here," Rax said to himself. "The little pet dog is outside and all by herself. No one here to protect her, to protect her from me." He chuckled.

With that Rax clung low to the ground, creeping his way up the garden fence towards the house. He carefully put one huge paw after another and instinctively crouched along trying not to be seen, as this is how coyotes sneak up on their prey. The prey this time was Pork Chop.

Pork Chop ran up to the door and frantically started pawing at the glass storm door. "Help, Help me. Please!" cried Pork Chop as loud as he could. *BARK! BARK! BARK!* She barked in her loudest voice, a very loud voice for a 7 pound dog.

Mr. Bear was baking something in the oven and didn't hear Pork Chop. He was busy making bread for dinner. He looked up through the window, but he didn't notice Rax, the Coyote, lying low in the brush along the fence.

Pork Chop pounded on the screen door with all of her might and yelled her loudest yell when finally Mr. Bear heard her.

"It's not time to come in yet, Pork Chop." Said Mr. Bear. "You need a good hour time out and it hasn't been 15 minutes yet."

"Help, Help!" screamed Pork Chop to Mr. Bear. "The coyote is going to get me! Rax is going to get me! Open the door, please, right now!" she begged.

Mr. Bear looked out into the yard, he could see nothing was there. He didn't see Rax hiding on his belly amongst the brown stalks and weeds.

"Quit making up stories and lying, Pork Chop." Said Mr. Bear. He was very annoyed, he had hoped Pork Chop would learn a lesson quickly; she was after all, a very smart dog.

Again, Pork Chop called out loud to Mr. Bear, "Can't you see the coyote? Rax, Mr. Bear," she exclaimed. She put her paws up on the glass and pushed back and forth, shaking the door.

Mr. Bear looking out the window for a second time and didn't see anything out of order, nothing looked strange about a dull, gray winter day. He was convinced that Pork Chop was trying to lie again.

Rax, meanwhile, was almost to the side of the house, Mr. Bear couldn't see him off the side, sneaking ever closer; thanking himself for his good luck. Pork Chop was just a leap away from him with no one to help her.

Pork Chop was terrified, she cried out for Big Riff, the one hundred pound German police dog. "Help Riff, Help Riff!" *WOOF! WOOF! WOOF!* She barked.

Riff was laying down by the fireplace in the house next door, he was almost asleep and very comfortably curled into a big ball of fur, his huge head resting on his paws. He heard nothing and finally went to sleep.

The coyote was ready to pounce. He could grab Pork Chop and run away in no time. Pork Chop was pounding on the door screaming for help "MR. BEAR, MR. BEAR!! PLEASE OPEN THE DOOR!!"

Mr. Bear rushed to the door to yell at Pork Chop and give her one more chance to quit telling lies. He yanked the handle and angrily pulled the door...

Rax was in mid-stride as he saw the door opening, he dodged in a circle to change direction and run away. Rax knew that someone was coming to help Pork Chop and that he needed to run away fast.

As Mr. Bear opened the door, he was shocked to see Pork Chop so afraid that she just leapt into his arms and started licking his face. "I'll never lie again, Mr. Bear. Never again. I promise." She cried real tears and Mr. Bear knew that she meant it. But just then, out the corner of his eye, Mr. Bear saw the ominous shape of a dog. A large dog. That was no dog at all, but a coyote, a big male coyote. Mr. Bear looked at the snow with the dog's tracks coming right to his door; he knew then, that Pork Chop was telling the truth and that she was in mortal danger.

Mr. Bear started to cry as he held Pork Chop tightly. Pork Chop was still crying but she was happy to be safe in Mr. Bear's arms. The two of them sat on the couch and watched the fire, and then went to sleep.

The End

Pork Chop and the Baby Deer

Volume 4

It was a late August day on Grosse Ile (The "Big Island" in French). Pork Chop was laying on the top of the couch, looking out the window. She liked to climb up on the top of the armrest and lay down with her paws resting her head. She would stretch out and gaze out the window at the river below. She liked to look at the boats in the water with all of the different colors and sizes. The river ran flat on some days and blustery with white caps the next. It didn't matter to Pork Chop, she was excited to see the river at all considering she stood barely over half of a foot tall and weighed six and a half pounds from her fluffy red cheeks to her upswept tail.

Pork Chop also liked the view in the back of the house, a small yard and garden that opened into the woods, the woods were thicker and darker as you got deeper into them; it was full of dark things too, like hawks and eagles, hungry raccoons, and worst of all for a small dog, coyotes!

Pork Chop went in the back of the house and climbed up on Mr. Bear's favorite chair, it was pork chops favorite chair too. She climbed up to the very top part of the back of the chair where she could look out into the backyard and see everything. All dogs are nosey; it's in their nature to be nosey; that's why dogs make such good watchdogs, and Pork Chop was no different, she liked to look out towards the woods and see what she could see.

Pork Chop scanned the backyard from side to side, there were the usual squirrels and various birds about the garden, doing what squirrels and birds do; Pork Chop just smiled and watched.

In the back of the yard, just behind the woods, was a huge red deer! He was the biggest deer Pork Chop ever saw. He had a big rack of horns on his head, Pork Chop counted ten full points and one little one on the left side. He was strolling through the edge of the woods without a care in the world, the "alpha" buck of the woods. (Alpha means head of the herd). He put his nose up to the wind and smelling something he didn't like, bolted back in the bush he strode out from.

Pork Chop was amazed! She watched the bucks white tail bouncing until it was out of sight. She couldn't wait to tell Mr. Bear about what she saw. She was just about to jump down off of the chair when she noticed two small brown lumps in the high grass behind the shed. She looked closer and the brown lumps moved! Pork Chop barked, but behind the glass window, only she could hear it.

The two lumps suddenly stood up, light brown bodies with white spots, a couple of fawns! Wow! Thought Pork Chop, first the 11 point buck and now the two baby deers. Little fawns. Pork Chop looked back and forth, she was trying to find the mother of the two fawns; but she was nowhere in sight. Why would the mama abandon the two baby deers, she thought

Just at that moment the door opened and Mr. Bear

was home. Pork Chop ran off the chair and ran breathlessly to her master. "Mr. Bear, Mr. Bear!" cried Pork Chop, "I saw a big, huge, buck and I saw two baby deers in the back of the shed," Pork Chop exclaimed.

"You saw the red buck did you, Pork Chop; he is huge indeed, well over three hundred pounds he is, and a huge rack on his head. When did you see him?" asked Mr. Bear.

"He was at the edge of the woods, but then he ran back the other way," Pork Chop exclaimed. "There were two baby deers in the brush too, they were little and they had white spots all over them."

"Pork Chop, the word is deer, not deers," Mr. Bear said. "I said that there were two of them, didn't I?" Two of them means deers." said Pork Chop.

From the back of the room came a rustling sound, then came little footsteps followed by laughter...it was baby Mason. He had awoke from his nap, his cornflower blue eyes sparkled when I've spied Pork Chop. Baby Mason loved Pork Chop and would follow her around the room wherever she went.

"Pork Chop, tell me about the fawns in the brush," asked Mr. Bear. There aren't supposed to be fawns this time of year. It's August, fawns are born in spring," he explained.

"Come look for yourself, Mr. Bear" and with that Pork Chop jumped up on the back of the chair, her nose pointing to the two small fawns lying in the weeds at the end of the garden.

"Well, I'll be darned," Mr. Bear said. "Two deer in our backyard, and only a couple of weeks old at that."

"No, Mr. Bear, its two deers, if it were one deer, it would be "deer," but two deer are "deers," like two dogs are dogs," explained Pork Chop.

"I'm sorry Pork Chop, but you are wrong. The plural of deer is the same as a single deer, or "deer." I know it's a little confusing, but you'll eventually understand." Mr. Bear said.

Baby Mason clamored up to the window ledge and pointed outside "deers, deers" he cried out and jumped up and down.

"See, Mr. Bear, Baby Mason agrees with me, it is "deers." laughed Pork Chop. "I can't wait to go outside and see the baby deers, Mr. Bear, I am going to protect them."

"No way Pork Chop, I don't want you anywhere near those fawns, I mean it; you stay clear of them for your own good." said Mr. Bear sternly.

Pork Chop sighed in agreement, she didn't want Mr. Bear mad at her, and she should obey. She spent the rest of the night playing with Mason until his dad, Mr. Bear's nephew, picked him up. Then they went to bed...

The next morning Pork Chop awoke to the bright sun shining through the windows in the back living room. She jumped up and ran to the chair to peer out into the garden, the fawns were gone.

Pork Chop wanted to help the baby deer so bad that

she couldn't stand it. She knew that Mr. Bear was very clear that she stay away from the fawns, but she wanted to go to them anyway.

Pork Chop ran out the door with Mr. Bear when he went out to work on his car. Mr. Bear was busy with his tools and didn't notice Pork Chop as she ran right down to the garden where the fawns had been yesterday.

Pork Chop looked around the garden and moved very slowly. She didn't want to scare the baby fawns. Back and forth, she swung her head peering through the stubble and weeds, past a huge pile of leaves and sticks. Then, at the edge of the garden in the bare spot on the ground, lay the two fawns wide eyed and motionless.

Pork Chop was amazed at their beauty; they both had coats of white spots on their backs, with reddish streaks of dark brown on both sides. Their noses were bright pink and they followed Pork Chops every move with their eyes.

"Don't worry littler deers, I will protect you." whispered the little dog. She immediately went on patrol at the edge of the garden, her head swinging back and forth, looking for danger.

No sooner had Pork Chop become the watch-dog for the fawns when danger did appear in the form of a huge, scraggly coyote named Rax, the apex predator. An apex predator means that Rax is the biggest, meanest coyote in the area; and yes, Rax was big and mean with a pointed nose and a mouth full of sharp teeth.

Rax started to scan the area when he spied Pork Chop at the edge of the garden. He could tell that Pork Chop was interested in something, but he could not see what it was. Rax sniffed the air for scent, arching his back and reaching his nose into the wind. No scent he thought. Except the dog. But what is the dog looking at thought Rax, his curiosity bringing him closer to the edge of the garden.

Suddenly, Pork Chop saw the familiar, mottled brown coat of Rax, the coyote. She ran back and forth across the garden fence barking, "Stay away Rax, Leave those baby deers alone," she growled with her harshest bark.

"Well, well, well," snarled Rax to Pork Chop. "If it isn't that little pet dog I hate so much." He said.

As Rax approached the garden he still hadn't noticed the two fawns, who froze completely still in the sight of such danger.

"What are you looking at, little dog? Growled Rax to Pork Chop. Who are you talking to?" Rax moved even closer until at the corner of the garden he saw the two fawns trembling in the weeds, shivering with fear, but; absolutely motionless.

"So this is what you're trying to hide, is it. A couple of tender, young deer." Rax couldn't believe his luck. He knew the little dog was hiding something, something like a new born fawn, something he couldn't smell because newborns have no scent.

Rax bounded over the fence while Pork Chop barked and ran furiously back and forth, unable to get past the fence.

The fawns bleated, crying as the big coyote approached them, they were terrified but were frozen still with fear.

Rax leapt over the pile of leaves and sticks as he prepared to grab the fawns when suddenly the garden exploded, a huge, red ball of fur erupted from under the pile of leaves, it was the giant red buck, his tail up in panic.

Rax tried to get out of his way but he wasn't fast enough, the buck lowered his head full of antlers and dug his hooves into the ground. The 300 pound buck sprang like lighting towards the coyote. To the buck, the coyote was an ancient enemy and he was fighting in a panic.

Rax tried to jump out of the way, but he couldn't escape the bucks' 11 point rack, no indeed as he flew through the air, thrown from the antlers. Rax rolled and tried to run but the buck was too quick and too strong, again Rax was propelled into the air, turning end over end, coming down on the other side of the fence, reeling in pain. He fled just as quickly as he came without looking back or thinking twice.

Pork Chop couldn't believe her eyes. Rax got a good beating; the two fawns were stumbling up the hill, their mother; the doe, was leading them away to safety. The huge buck bounded into the woods in a flash and Pork Chop was all alone.

At least she thought she was all alone until she looked and saw Mr. Bear, and he was not happy.

"Pork Chop," Mr. Bear said in a deep, serious voice. "I told you to stay away from the fawns didn't I?" "Those fawns were perfectly safe, the mother was in the background to help them but you jumped in there and the coyote was attracted to you, he sensed you were protecting something. You almost caused those fawns their lives because you didn't listen. But, while I am mad, I am very proud of you to stand up to Rax like you did, you are a very good watch dog, Pork Chop."

As they walked up to the house Pork Chop looked back into the woods and saw a red shadow in the distance. The big, red buck had saved everyone from Rax, he was truly the king of the forest.

The End

Pork Chop and the Baby Panda Bear
Volume 5

It was summertime in Grosse Ile, the "Big Island" in French. Pork Chop was all excited because the day came that she waited all week for. Today, Mr. Bear was going to take her to the zoo.

Pork Chop liked all of the animals at the zoo, she liked the different colored birds, the lions and tigers and bears; but what she really came to see was the panda bear exhibit.

The panda bear exhibit was the most popular in the zoo. Brought in about ten years ago and given a large amount of space in which to grow on, the zoo built the exhibit into one of the best in the country.

Pork Chop ran ahead, she was filled with the excitement of actually being at the park. Pork Chop liked to smell the smells of the zoo. She could smell the hotdogs, the hamburgers, and the ribs.

Dogs smell things much better and much differently than people, Pork Chop could smell the cotton candy and caramel apples on a stick.

"I told you not to run ahead of us Pork Chop, I don't want to have to look for you all afternoon," said Mr. Bear loudly. "I want you to stay close, and for heaven's sake don't try to open every door, and test every gate."

Pork Chop was way ahead of him, jumping down the main boulevard towards the panda bear hall. She walked up to the front of the exhibit and tried to see over the big rocks that guard the moat that surrounds the hall.

Pork Chop could see the bigger male panda bears, but she didn't see any mothers and their babies. The males stayed on the one side of the enclosure, up in the higher rocks of the habitat. She strained to get up on the wall, to get a better look; but she just wasn't satisfied with her view.

Pork Chop jumped down and ran all around the exhibit. She was trying to get into the hall to get as close to the panda bears as she could.

While Pork Chop was looking for a new way in, inside the enclosure, Mr. Wynn; the caretaker for the panda bears, was getting ready to go home from his shift. It was important that he left the zoo before nightfall, as you see; Mr. Wynn was nearsighted. His eyes were so bad that without glasses, he could barely see.

Meanwhile, Mr. Bear was frantically looking around for Pork Chop. He checked the monkey exhibit first, Pork Chop could spend hours looking and talking with the monkeys.

Mr. Bears face was bright red in color, he was sweating heavily and he was out of breath. There was so many people and kids at the park he didn't know where to look any more. He had been to the loin's exhibit, the polar bear exhibit, and the tropical bird sanctuary, but Pork Chop was nowhere to be found.

Back at the panda bear exhibit the caretaker, Mr.

Wynn, was fumbling with his keys in a dark corner of the exhibit, Pork Chop was fumbling with a latch on a newly found door. As Pork Chop wiggled the door, Mr. Wynn grabbed his keys, "Seems like that strange sound is coming from this door." he thought.

Pork Chop heard Mr. Wynn's keys through the steel door. She jumped up on her hind legs and scratched at the door. Mr. Wynn heard the scratching from inside the enclosure; he put the right key into the lock and turned, as he pulled the door firmly, Pork Chop came tumbling into the panda bear enclosure!

Mr. Wynn jumped at the sight of Pork Chop and jerked straight up; as he did, his glasses popped off his head and dropped to the ground, shattering them. He was nearly blind without them. "What is that little furry thing on the ground," he thought.

Mr. Wynn looked down at Pork Chop, but all he could see was a ball of black and white fuzz, "it's a baby panda bear" exclaimed Mr. Wynn out loud. "I didn't know the females were expecting."

Mr. Wynn gently laid Pork Chop on a large, flat boulder that was part of the exhibit. He didn't want to get between the baby cub and its mother, or worse, his father. He quietly stepped backwards out of the door and closed it shut until it locked.

Pork Chop was locked in the panda bear exhibit with all of the panda bears. There were three large, male panda bears at the top of the exhibit, three young, female panda bears playing together at the opposite end and an older, large female that sat in between.

Pork Chop slowly stood up and walked towards the middle of the enclosure; as she did the big male panda bears moved the same way. Pork Chop moved three more feet away and the large male panda bears moved again, and then they started to come towards her growling and shaking their heads.

Pork Chop turned around, hoping to see the zoo keeper Mr. Wynn. He was nowhere in sight as he was off to tell everybody the good news! The zoo had a new baby panda bear! A black and white bundle of joy.

The big males were moving even closer and closer towards Pork Chop. She was starting to realize that she could be in real danger. "I should have listened to Mr. Bear and not got lost," she said.

Just as the male panda bears reached Pork Chop, the big female panda bear ran up to her and cradling her in her arms, she growled and hissed back at the three male bears. She climbed to the opposite side of the enclosure and held Pork Chop close to her body, as if to protect her.

Just then, Mr. Bear frantically searching for Pork Chop looked into the panda bear enclosure with both horror and surprise. There in front of him and a small but growing crowd was Pork Chop, up on the cliffs of the enclosure, being held in the arms of a three hundred pound bear.

"Don't panic Pork Chop!" yelled Mr. Bear. "I will get some help!" Before Mr. Bear could go and get help, the zookeeper Mr. Wynn and the whole zoo staff were running up to see the new baby panda bear.

The zookeeper pointed up at Pork Chop nestled in the arms of the female and exclaimed "will you look at that, the mother and baby are doing just fine."

The rest of the staff looked up to what was to them, a small Pomeranian dog. She sure was black and white but, she was no baby panda bear.

The zookeeper and the staff entered the panda bear exhibit and lured the female away from Pork Chop with a bunch of bananas.

After a lot of promising that Pork Chop would not repeat his mistake, the zoo staff returned Pork Chop to Mr. Bear. He was angry that she didn't listen to him in the first place.

On the way home from the zoo, Pork Chop fell asleep on the seat, her head resting on Mr. Bears leg. She had one heck of an exciting day, Mr. Bear smiled then sighed, knowing how lucky he was that the little dog wasn't hurt. He thought to himself, "Only Pork Chop, my little Pork Chop, could cause so much commotion for such a small, little dog.

The End

Pork Chop: The Pluckey, Pomeranian Puppy

Jerry J. Carducci was born in Ecorse, Michigan on July 10, 1954. He was educated at the St. Francis Xavier grade school by the Sisters of St. Joseph, the University of Detroit High School and the University of Detroit (BBA 1979) both run by the Jesuits. He also attended Western Michigan University in Kalamazoo, Michigan.

After a career in large companies, Jerry along with longtime business partner, Phillip Clervi, ran a small trailer hitch shop in Southgate, Michigan, a downriver suburb. Many of the characters in Jerry's writings are gleaned from thirty plus years of dealing with the public.

Jerry Carducci lives on an island in the middle of the Detroit river, between the south end of downriver and Canada. He lives there with his lovely wife of forty-two years, Carmel Elaine, and their dog, "Pork Chop", a Plucky, Pomeranian puppy.

Other books by Jerry Carducci includes the five volume set, "Pork Chop the Plucky, Pomeranian Puppy, currently available exclusively on Kindle, soon to be a print edition for Amazon. Jerry's seventh book, "The Mill", a novel that starts in 929 A.D. and ends in 1974 is scheduled for publication in early 2018.

Made in the USA
Middletown, DE
02 September 2020

17988604R10028